Crop Circles

A Seed Keeper Novella, Volume 1

Cathy Smith

Published by Cathy Smith, 2022.

CROP CIRCLES

First edition. July 20, 2022.

Copyright © 2022 Cathy Smith.

ISBN: 979-8230039310

Written by Cathy Smith.

Table of Contents

Chapter 1-The Pitch

Felix could smell Marcus's increased perspiration. He knew this upcoming pitch was Marcus's passion project. But he couldn't help but wonder whether Marcus wanted more than a big commission?

"Our pitch is solid. You have nothing to worry about." Felix patted him on the shoulder. There were people who thought the short, hairy man was creepy, but his kind was more touchy than most. He could've used his holomask to make his human simulation to be more attractive. Though he preferred to be "hairy" if he couldn't be furry. Thankfully, he wore a flea collar to keep the fleas away.

"Under normal circumstances, but I have to pitch to Lee Astor," Marcus spat out the man's name as if it were an expletive.

Felix cackled. "Don't worry. He's only passing through. You'll outlast him and can wait until the next Director of the Terran branch of Agristar is assigned to the system. The next one may be receptive."

Marcus swallowed. "I won't have to wait out Lee Astor if we're successful. I'll be able to pass through Terra myself."

***

They played videos of Terran athletes engaged in competition on the smart screen. Lee watched the video and said, "Do you plan to use these Terran celebrities for endorsements?"

Felix's ears twitched as he heard Marcus grind his teeth. They'd supplied Lee with the notes for their presentation. The fact he didn't know who these athletes were showed he hadn't reviewed the notes.

"All these athletes have chronic diseases. The ice skater has asthma. The cyclist muscular dystrophy. The swimmer-"

Marcus gulped. "The swimmer has diabetes."

"Diabetes? Isn't that what happens when a Terran gets too obese?" Lee sniffed in distaste. He brought up an image of a fat Terran eating a pizza pie and wings by themselves.

"It's little wonder they get diseased if they don't have imperial fitness standards."

Marcus switched back to the athletes. "These Terrans have as much discipline as any Imperial. Yet they still have chronic health conditions."

"That is unfortunate. Are you going to suggest we donate to them for good PR?"

Felix's ears twitched in annoyance. *He didn't even read the executive summary of our presentation or else he'd know what we're driving at.*

"I'm suggesting that these Terrans lead productive lives despite their disabilities. This is because of Terran medical technology and treatments for chronic health conditions. I'm proposing we extract their chronic care technology and treatments to imperial space." He had to enunciate his words carefully, so he didn't clench his teeth.

Lee remained silent for a long moment, and then he frowned. "Do we want to enable unhealthy lifestyles and propagate unfit genes in the Empire?"

He pounded his hand on the desk. "No, it's not worth extracting this medical technology to imperial space. There's no demand for accommodation to subpar genes."

Marcus frowned. "The Empire's stigmatization of chronic conditions means there's a vast underserved population."

"The Overseers extracted prime physical specimens from Terra. They bred our ancestors for optimum health. We don't have as many genetic defects as Terrans do," Lee said.

Marcus snorted. "Yet, no one dares to mention arranged marriages nowadays, or you'll have a rebellion on your hands. Imperials from the Human Sector aren't as selective as they used to be."

Lee raised his brow. "Are you inferring that genetic defects have entered the imperial bloodlines? Our customers will resent the inference. And there's no use insulting them for a medical technology that hasn't been perfected."

"The Terrans work on a continuous improvement premise. Insulin was discovered over 100 years ago, and they've built on it since then. The life expectancy of a diabetic was 15 years at the most—"

Lee sniffed. "We're still more disciplined and selective than the Terrans are. It's little wonder they had to create chronic care. They have defectives who should be culled out of the gene pool."

Marcus's knuckles turned white on his laser pointer. "Culled? You mean the genocide of anyone with less than perfect genes?"

"I'm not suggesting an extermination program. Let nature take its course and let the fittest survive."

Lee waved his hand. "Anyone who needs diabetic treatments can immigrate to the Terran System."

Marcus's back stiffened, and the color rose in his cheeks. His Adam's apple bobbed as he gulped before he spoke. "We could make them aware of the treatments and charge to transport them here."

"Huh?"

"If we won't export diabetic supplies to the Empire, we can import Imperial patients. We can charge them for vetting the treatments and their providers."

Lee waved his hands. "There would be too little demand to justify the expenditure."

Which was the signal Felix needed in order to speak up. "There are non-human Imperials who would also be a market for medical tourism. Earth's veterinarians also offer comprehensive care for Earth's animal population. I know that they offer a complete wellness program for felines."

Lee looked at him. "That explains a lot. However, such medical tourism won't be workable. Not while the Overseers advocate an acclimatization program for the Terrans. Only human imperials are allowed on Earth. Should the Overseers reevaluate Earth's status, we'll reevaluate your pitch, not before then."

"Then why don't we do discreet extractions?" Felix asked.

"Discrete extractions?" said Lee, as if he didn't think Felix knew what it was.

"Get samples of the diabetic supplies and veterinary drugs. Do a thorough screening. Hire people from Terra capable of administering the treatments."

Lee snorted. "Only the Freetraders have an Insiders program."

"Then poach one of them that suits our needs," Marcus slammed his right fist into his hand as he said this.

Lee snorted at the thought of this. "They are unnecessary. There's no way we can get worker visas for them."

***

Felix's tail drooped while Marcus's back was ramrod straight after the conference. He strode out with footsteps that were heavier than usual for him.

"He can't wait for his next promotion, but lacks the vision needed to innovate in this company. Planets' status gets reevaluated all the time. It's possible to get a re-evaluation if they're shown to have a commodity required in imperial space." Marcus muttered.

"You know that, but won't let yourself be promoted off Terra. I hope she's worth it," Felix said.

Marcus glanced at him. "She?"

"I assume you've got personal reasons for wanting to stay in the system," Felix shrugged.

Marcus rubbed his forehead. "Yes, I do, and I can't disclose it without giving people too much leverage over me."

Chapter 2-Crop Circle

Akweks Pine never had to pay for a tabloid. Not when his grandfather filled his newsfeed with ridiculous clickbait. Teaching Totah media literacy took a great deal of patience. Totah would've considered the Magpie a yellow rag if they had a print edition. However, he became more credulous about what was on his feed when it was shared by his friends.

Worse yet, The Magpie was a local publication. This made Totah think he should support a local business. It was chock-full of indigenous conspiracy theories.

Totah was the one who brought the crop circles on the Rez to Akweks's attention. He forwarded the article to his newsfeed. Akweks recognized the farmer in the picture as one of Totah's acquaintances.

Akweks: Isn't that Al? It's about time The Magpie wrote a proper news article.

Totah: It's about Al's crop circles.

Akweks: I'm glad Indigenous food sovereignty is getting the attention it deserves. Though I hope The Magpie's rep for weird news won't be bad PR for the cause.

Totah: Click the link, and you'll see what I mean.

Akweks did so and found a series of images of peculiar symbols worked within a cornfield. *Will our Rez be the point of First Contact?* The article began.

Akweks: I can't believe they're getting elders involved in their yellow journalism.

Totah: Al says The Magpie was the only newspaper willing to report on this.

Akweks: It's probably the Rez's ATVers getting creative. They're always tearing up the local cornfields.

Indeed, they had similar problems with the field between their houses. Totah gave him land to build a house close to his residence and owned an acre between their houses, too.

Totah: Why don't we go over to Al's before we assume ATVs made the circles?

Which became an outing. Perhaps seeing this turned into clickbait would stop Totah from being so credulous.

***

Totah tried to phone Al, but Al left a message on his voicemail and refused to answer his phone. "No, we're not open to visitors or journalists. We don't want any trespassing."

Akweks hoped that would be the end of it, but Totah reached Al through a private message on his feed. *I'll make an exception for you and your grandson if you want to stop by.*

Akweks rolled his eyes at this.

***

There were footsteps in the field visible from the laneway when Akweks drove to Al's farm. "See, humans vandalized it, not aliens." He said to Totah.

Totah grunted something in response. He spoke more clearly when he saw Al waiting for them.

"Where's the crop circles everyone's talking about?" Totah asked Al.

Al snorted. "I wished I'd kept it to myself and didn't talk to the Magpie. I wound up with a lot of tourists coming to my field. They caused even more damage than the crop circles did."

"I let them in at the beginning, but now I'm posting 'Keep Out' signs. They keep tearing them down."

"You should've charged them a higher fee to cover the damages." Totah spoke up.

Al's brows came together. "Charge the tourists? Do you think it'll work?"

Akweks held up three fingers and listed three likely outcomes to this maneuver.

"I figure three things can happen."

He brought down one raised finger. "The tourists take your offer at face value, and you get a proper cut of the tourist dollars. Why should the hotels and restaurants get all the money when you and your field don't?"

He pulled the second finger down. "We get into subtle psychology with the second and third."

"Psychology?" Al and Totah asked him.

"Think of it as reverse psychology. They ignore the keep out sign. But putting up a sign charging them fees discourages the cheap. You won't need to tell them 'no' outright."

Al snorted. "I'd rather drive them away with the pellet gun I use to scare away the crows."

"Then you'll end up in trouble for using excessive force." Akweks said, shaking out his hand at a memory and losing the visual track of his points.

Al glanced at Totah. "He knows from experience."

"What's the third scenario?" Al asked him.

"You make the smart people think you're running a tourist trap. They'll stay away and encourage everyone else, too."

Totah frowned. "The tourist trap idea wouldn't work. You'd need to commit to the idea to create that impression."

"Commitment?" Akweks asked.

"Tacky souvenirs and signage."

"There's some print on demand services you can use to create tacky merchandise with no money down." Akweks shrugged.

"But they expect to get paid eventually, right?" Al said.

"They get a commission if one of your products are ordered online. Create an online store with crop circle products with poor designs. It'll convince people you're trying to scam them. Then you can quietly shut it down when interest dies off."

Totah shrugged. "Posting 'stay away' on the feeds should be enough."

"I did that already, and it didn't help. I'll try the tacky tourist trap approach. My relatives do beadwork. I can tell them to make bad designs that are exploitative and set up an online shop for me."

*****

Of course, nothing worked out as planned. Akweks saw the follow-up when Totah forwarded Al's posts to his feed.

First came the T-shirts that sold out fast.

Then his relatives beaded keychains and medallions in the crop circle design. They became bestsellers.

Anyone who couldn't afford to see the crop circles in person could buy the souvenirs.

*****

One day Totah came to Akweks. He said, "A company sent Al a cease and desist letter for trademark infringement."

"Trademark infringement? Didn't he have the design for all these souvenirs from the crop circles that were in his field?""

Totah nodded "yes" at this.

"See what happens when he threatens to counter-sue them for damages to his cornfield. If those designs belong to them, then they must be the ones responsible for vandalizing his corn." Akweks told him.

As Akweks suspected, the sender of the cease and desist letter backed off. Al almost made enough money with the souvenirs to offset the damage in his field.

The remaining corn grew without interference once people had to pay to see the crop circles. Al took a precaution to keep the rest of the corn intact. He created a path to the crop circles and told the tourists not to step anywhere else.

Akweks suggested it to him. "Tell them, it's maintaining the circles. You won't be able to tell the circles from the path beaten by the nosy. Not if they keep walking through the field and creating new paths."

Eventually the harvest time came. Al gathered all the still standing corn stalks which ended the crop circles. When he finished harvesting, the circles were gone.

"I recouped my losses with the tourist dollars. Though I prefer a regular yield of corn rather than crop circles." Al said.

He commemorated the end of tourist season by having a sale of pouches of seed corn grown in the field.

Grow your own crop circle, was the tagline.

"He shouldn't promise that they'll have crop circles, too. They'll end up calling him out for false advertising if it doesn't happen," Akweks said.

Of course, Totah fell for this constant advertisement. "I'd like to try it out to see if it happens if we grow some of Al's seed corn."

"Regular seed corn should do. Don't pay Al's prices. You might even pick it up for free from the Indigenous Seedkeeper's group." Akweks said.

Of course, it became his duty to purchase the seed corn. They planted the corn on the acre between their houses.

"What are we going to do with a field of corn? You'd be better off keeping the seeds that can fit in the garden."

"Aliens can't make crop circles in gardens. I need a field for that." Totah said.

"What if they don't come? Are you going to keep on trying until they do?" Akweks asked.

"I'll try it for a year," Totah said.

It was times like this that Akweks wished he could just tell his grandfather "no." "You would be better off expecting to grow corn instead of crop circles. A garden is one thing. What do you expect to do with a field full of corn?"

"I can always give the extra seeds to the Seedkeepers. The extra cobs can go to the longhouse for their ceremonies," Totah replied.

"Then you better make sure that you choose white corn for your seed corn. They won't accept anything else."

Chapter 3-Overnight Flights

The Rez supplied Totah with a new drama to capture his attention. As usual, Totah forwarded his concerns over to Akweks in his feed. It was a picture of a light in the sky.

The caption stated: *Why does the government fly planes over the Rez at night?*

Al's comment was, *Maybe it's the Star People coming back.*

Someone's comment that, *it's probably the government being nosy*, went viral.

Akweks expected the trend to pass, like everyone's interest in the crop circles was gone.

Totah still had white corn growing on his acre plot, but his friends' requests for free corn and updates on its progress made him forget about the crop circles. Indeed, he preferred a proper harvest unimpeded by damages. Though the ATVers had other ideas.

The ATVers had been there all along, but neither he nor Totah had cared about the tracks back when it was an empty field. However, their riding was now damaging the corn crop.

When he mentioned it to Totah he said, "They shouldn't expect me to keep this field empty to please them. My white corn does more good than their ATVs do."

Indeed, they followed Haudenosaunee practice and started harvesting it during the green corn ceremony. The cobs weren't mature yet, but were edible. Totah allowed his friends to harvest two bushels to make green corn soup for the longhouse ceremony in the spring, and they'd shared some of it with them.

They left the rest to mature in the field and Totah regarded the damages left by ATV tracks like a mother dealing with infant mortality. One morning, he was particularly upset when he saw the newest tracks in the field. "Do other rural areas have to put up with ATVers wrecking their fields and the government flying aircraft over their airspace? It can't be good for the crops."

"Maybe the government wildlife agency is doing an aerial survey? We have the largest tract of Carolinian forest in North America."

"They are mandated to have the courtesy to give us a warning before they do things like that," Totah said.

Akweks kept expecting the local newspapers to print a notice about an aerial survey, but it didn't happen. Though the complaints of the overnight lights persisted on the online feeds.

Maybe it's lights reflected from those new internet satellites that billionaire is putting out? Someone said online.

We'd hear about this in the night sky of the entire province, not just the Rez.

More videos of the lights occurred and someone said, *This is getting ridiculous. I'm going to buy one of those laser pointers to protest if they won't stay out of our airspace.*

The suggestion went viral in NDN digital country. *They won't leave us alone, so we won't let them fly in our airspace in peace.*

To make matters worse, Totah discovered this new fad. He called Akweks over to his place to show him his latest drop shipment. He had it laid out on the dinnertable for Akweks to review.

"What is this?" It looked like a chrome pen, but he knew Totah wouldn't call him because of that.

"It's for stopping those government airplanes from snooping over our field. They've changed from flying overhead to hovering over cornfields. Now everyone wants to use laser pointers to disrupt the flights.."

Akweks shook his head "It can't be legal to disrupt airplane pilots' navigation."

"They didn't ask for the elected or traditional council's permission to fly in our airspace. I figure they have no right to complain about what we're doing," Totah retorted.

Seeing that Totah's mind was made up, Akweks changed tactics. "Then I'll keep it on hand in case they come swooping over our field."

Totah delegated most work to Akweks, so he let him have the laser pointer. The entire plan was to keep the laser pointer so Totah forgot about it and then sell it in the online marketplace. He found it was best not to tell Totah "no" outright, but to direct his attention elsewhere.

He also thought it would be a good idea to ask the councils if they would do something about these overnight flights. Was it possible that they'd forgotten to notify the community about an initiative?

***

The elected council sent out a notice that they hadn't approved the overnight flights and were sending a letter to the provincial and federal governments to put an end to them. It took the traditional council longer to respond but they said the same thing in a public notice by their preferred newspaper. They also couldn't figure out what was going on.

"We have the traditional and elected councils arguing who should run the Rez. I would support any council that knows what's going on with those overnight flights. You have that laser pointer on hand, don't you?" Totah asked him as he studied both newspapers with these notices.

"Yeah, yeah." He knew he better keep the pointer to act as Totah's security blanket, or it'd escalate to where he'd be ordering a bazooka online to shoot the planes down next.

He wouldn't be surprised if this was some elaborate hoax. Of course, there was some video evidence of the flights, but he never saw any in person. Had someone made a video that went viral and everybody was making up those videos to get part of the action? He figured all they needed to produce one video was a flashlight in a dark room. Supposedly, the flights took place at night and the aircraft were moving so fast that all you could see were the headlights.

***

One night, Akweks had a hard time sleeping because of the light in the field he thought was coming from the ATV riders. Their motors had a high pitch that could not be good. He assumed it was like the Rez cars. They worked but were not in top condition.

It was one thing to keep the car after it got a few dents. But some of these owners neglected basic self-care for their cars and ran them into the ground because they were too cheap to pay for proper maintenance. He opened his window to see a bunch of lights in the field.

"It has to be the ATVers," said Akweks.

He was tempted to reach for his pellet gun but was afraid the Rez would say that it was overkill. But then, the rest of the Rez didn't have to worry about repeat offenders coming back to vandalize and make noises near their home.

He tried to use his cell phone to call the police, but the signal was dead. This kind of stuff happened on his reserve so that it didn't shock him but was annoying. "It's too bad I got rid of the landline. Totah keeps his just for this occasion, but I got tired of paying the extra expense for mine."

He gritted his teeth as that whining grew louder and louder, like nails on a chalkboard to his sleep-deprived brain.

He turned on a light in his home to get that pellet gun. However, he saw Totah's laser pointer instead. "Hm." He picked it up, and after a moment's thought, pocketed it.

Though he cast a glance at the pellet gun. "You're still my last resource if I need it."

The pellet gun could take out most of the wild animals here, but should give humans a small sting as long as it wasn't used near them. These ATVers were sure to have families who would complain if their babies were hurt, but didn't do anything to keep their babies in line and out of mischief.

He left his house and went to the edge of his grass where the field began. The lights in his field swarmed in weird patterns as if they were a synchronized swimming team. Akweks didn't think it was anything other than an attempt to induce a headache in him.

He met the biggest light with a beam from the laser pointer. It shuddered and turned orange as if in alarm. Then he repeated the pattern with all the other lights, and they all went still as if they had been paralyzed.

He indicated the direction he wanted them to go, which was on the road and off his property. All the lights blinked from orange to yellow to white. They followed the trail he had drawn with the laser, but when he got to the road, they climbed up instead of on the road.

Akweks blinked. Then he shrugged. *Don't tell me they're using drones in the fields now. I thought that was only happening in the main village of the Rez.*

The Rez was slightly behind, but not entirely out of the loop of the new technology that was going on in the mainstream. He should check and ask people for their opinion on the feeds in the morning.

Chapter 4-Deniability

Akweks logged into his feed. He found the community bulletin board, so he could ask a question in that group: *Does anyone know if there are people using air drones in the fields?*

The comments filled up quickly:

Rez Scone: I keep seeing them in the village early in the morning. They like to take them out then to avoid the danger of anyone stealing them.

Akweks: I saw a bunch of lights in my cornfield and used my laser pointer to distract them.

Rez Scone: What if they weren't drones?

Akweks: What else could they be?

Rez Scone: Aliens.

Akweks: I saw a bunch of lights in the night sky above my cornfield. It could have been anything, but I suppose it was something from this world, like drones.

Rez Scone: Why don't you check to see if there's anything in your field leftover from your visitors?

Akweks: Do you think they left garbage and tracks in my field again?

Rez Scone: if it was aliens, they wouldn't leave garbage, but they would leave crop circles.

Akweks: I would consider a crop circle as much of an act of vandalism as track marks on my field by earthly ATV riders.

Rez Scone: Yeah but were where would you serve the subpoena if it were aliens?

Akweks didn't have a quick comeback, so he tried out the advice. *Let's see if there's anything suspicious in the field.*

***

There was a popcorn smell in the air as soon as he walked into the corn field. "Humph."

The smell grew more distinct when he got into the middle of the field. There were indentions and the cornstalks that were laid flat. It looked like someone had tried to lay a pattern in the field.

Popcorn disrupted the pattern on the ground. The shift from indentions to popcorn was sudden. He figured this must have been triggered when he disrupted the lights with the laser pointer. The popcorn trail path led off the field, towards the road and ended there.

He checked out the indentions in the cornstalks and realized it was akin to Al's crop circles.

I didn't even get a regular crop circle. I got a funky one.

***

Of course, Totah called Al over to look at the crop circle. "It's too bad your grandson wrecked the circle before it was complete."

Totah nodded agreement at this while Akweks rolled his eyes. "I don't consider it an honor to be vandalized, even if it was done by an alien."

"It's not vandalism. It's an attempt to communicate with us," Al said.

Akweks sniffed. "They should think of better ways to communicate with us rather than messing up our fields. So far, I just want to tell them to go home."

"Careful, language like that makes you sound like a right-winger," Al said.

"It'd be a shame to let xenophobia get in the way of first contact," he added.

Akweks snorted. "We have already had a first contact, and this has not worked well for the Onkwehon: we. These aliens seem to be as bad as the first settlers were."

Totah spoke up. "I'm sure aliens would have more to offer us than blankets full of smallpox."

"Yeah, right? They'd offer their version of beads and trinkets. Then expect us to sell out our land and resources for a pittance," Akweks retorted.

"You shouldn't have a negative attitude about this. Your rudeness will stop them from coming back," Al began.

Akweks gestured to the damages in the field. "It's not like I want to invite them back after what they did to my field."

"We can always recoup our expenses by making this a tourist spot like Al did when it happened on his farm," Totah said.

Akweks considered and then smirked. "Do you think we'd get a cease and desist letter from that company that tried to send it to Al? Once we get their contact information, we can trace them and sue for the damages."

***

So, Akweks took pictures of the cornfield to show the crop circles. He even put together bags of popcorn, which must be stale and dirty now to act like souvenirs. Then he created an online page to see if it'd get that company's attention.

"I don't know why you bother doing this," Totah said. "The people who sent that message to Al are probably hoaxsters."

"What if they are more devoted to their hoax than you think? What if they're the ones who created the crop circles to begin with?" Akweks asked him.

"Then they'd be idiots for claiming you infringed on their trademark. You could look it up on the government database. They'd have to leave their contact information there, and you'd know who you could sue."

Akweks's eyes widened. "You know you might have a good idea. I should check the trademark database to see if they registered the crop circle designs to anyone. Waiting for them to administer a copyright strike would take too long."

"If there is any such thing as copyright for these crop circles, then it will not be on Earth."

Except there was a problem when Akweks looked up the government database. It used text-based keywords. He knew what the images looked like, but he didn't know what they called them. The best he could think of was to look under the word "crop circle."

There were no entries under that keyword, but it showed him a list of words to use for related searches. They were agricultural corporations with registered trademarks. Of course, the larger ones took most of the trademarks, but there were smaller businesses as well. One particular term, 'Agristar', caught his eye.

The results were alphabetical. Perhaps it was just luck. Either that or the company wanted to rank at the top of search results. However, the word Agristar sounded like it'd have crop circles as part of their design. Either way, he clicked the link to the company's web page.

The first thing to greet him on the site was a series of crop circles which represented their logo design. He chuckled when he saw this. "Gotcha."

He looked for and found the contact information. This led to a feedback section which was formatted as a template to contact them. It even had a widget for uploading picture files. He preferred doing major research on a laptop, even though he had a smartphone with data. However, he still had pictures of crop circles from his and Al's fields on the phone. He used Bluetooth to save them onto the laptop's drive. Then he uploaded the package from the drive onto the contact form as a file.

There was a problem with formatting the question on the drop-down list of the subject line. He had to choose "other." *I saw these crop circles, and they look like your company logo. Are you responsible for this vandalism of me and my friend's cornfields?*

He did this out of nothing but due diligence. He figured they'd dismiss him as a crank. At the most, he expected them to deny they had anything to do with this. Claim it was a prankster who did this, if they acknowledged him at all.

Akweks got a reply the next day. He read it twice in disbelief at its wording.

Cease and desist this slander against our company. Should you continue to slander us, we will press charges for harassment.

It was more like they were supposed to tell whoever did this to cease and desist. If anything, he expected them to deny having anything to do with it. Maybe thank him for alerting them to the misuse of their logo.

He was tempted to send a response, but decided he needed more back up documentation, so he made up a script for an online video he intended to upload:

Whoever did this also did the crop circles in Al's field. There are probably more people like us.

I'll try to see what's happening locally first to see if any other fields had similar crop circles. Then I'll use the Internet to look things up in a wider circle. This company is defensive. It's like they're guilty of that, and they're trying to deny it.

It would have been smarter to deny all this and pretend a local hoaxster did this. Maybe even promise me they would investigate this. Claim that these crop circles were an unethical breach of their copyright design. They didn't do that, which I find suspicious.

Chapter 5-The Video

It was fortunate that Akweks and his grandfather had a system for gardening videos.

He showed up at Totah's place and handed Totah his phone, which had the best specs of either of their phones. Totah's cellphones were always two models out of date. He kept his phones until they stopped being supported. Akweks thought he was lucky to have gotten Totah to use smartphones at all.

Most times he was the one filming Totah giving gardening instructions and tips.

Totah was an active member of the Indigenous Seedkeepers group on the Rez. They got more people engaged by giving them videos to watch. Of course, in-person visitations were preferred for instructing the next generation of gardeners. Though that wasn't always possible. There was a chance the videos could intrigue someone enough to seek them out for a private session. This made Totah willing to learn how to make uploadable videos for the group.

This time Akweks said, "I want you to record me and the crop circles."

Totah frowned. "Do you really want people to find out about this? You have no proof other than this field and there is always someone who will say you faked it."

"I want to explain what happened. It's easier to get them to listen to me talking during a video than to read a wall of text online. Besides, it will be no worse than what Al did when he got crop circles in his field."

Totah grunted and followed him out into the field.

He kept his grandson in view as Akweks spoke.

Akweks wanted a video of himself so that he could post it online on his feed. He showed himself and his field with the messed up crop circles. And explained the situation surrounding their appearance:

"I heard a loud noise at night and saw lights in my field. I thought this was nothing more than kids riding around on their ATVs.

It messes up the crops, but it happens around here. Thinking about what was happening made me mad. But rather than reach for my pellet gun, I took out a laser pointer to psych them out."

He showed what he meant by showing his laser pointer and turning it on. Then he pointed it to the centre of the crop circle.

"Now, remember, this was all happening at night. All I could make up were lights I assumed were headlights. The laser pointer made the lights stop moving for a bit."

They went from white to yellow to orange to red the longer that I pointed it at them.

I pointed them to the path to the road to show them I wanted them to leave. They followed my instructions. But once they got to the road, the lights flew straight up."

He waved his pointer to show the motion.

"It was night, and I was just glad they left. I didn't think to do any more than that. I just headed off for bed."

"I checked for damages to my field the next morning when there was light out. Instead of having ATV tracks, I found these crop circles."

"They're not as pretty or detailed as some others."

He had left popcorn in the field to show where they had gone. "This is the trail they left when I motioned for them to hit towards the road.

Right now, all I can give you are videos of the consequences of that incident. Many people will think that I staged it. It didn't occur to me to record it on video at the time it was happening.

My crop circle is broken. I know it's messed up and not their original design. I know this since there's another farmer on my Rez who had crop circles in his field last year.

Some of you may even know his name because he turned it into a tourist spot. Eventually, he harvested the corn that he had in the field in the fall. However, it's still possible to look up the pictures taken of the crop circles when they were on his land.

It looks like whoever did this wanted to repeat the design in my field. My laser pointer distracted them and stopped them from doing this.

I don't think aliens did this.

When my friend capitalized on the crop circles in his field, he got a cease and desist letter. A company that claimed he infringed on their trademark.

I told him to threaten to counter-sue them since they made damages to his field. This made them drop it.

But then I get these circles in my field. And I looked up that company to see if they had registered the trademark. Or was it just someone trying to scam him for money?

So I went to see if their crop circle design actually had a trademark. I found a database and traced it to some agricompany. I had no way of knowing if they had anything to do with crop circles. Someone else could've copied the design. Yet, I sent them a picture of my crop circle and asked them what they wanted to do about it.

I know for a fact that the people who made these crop circles did it in at least two fields on my reserve. Has anyone else had circles in their field like this or lights in the sky happening close by?"

Chapter 6- The Video Goes Viral

Lee Astor didn't enjoy coming to the boondocks for meetings. However, it was part of the agricultural business. He couldn't always count on being able to serve his time in a sanitary vertical farm or farm factory. Especially if he was going to find new seeds worth extracting into imperial space.

Trina looked him in the eye. The bioluminescent glow of her eyes became apparent because of her annoyance. Though she could pass as human most times. "We need a record of all the fields you've done extractions from. A video has gone viral from an extraction site."

"Those Terran social media streams are a time sink." Lee waved his hand.

"The videos supply the information we need about their culture and their languages. You shouldn't dismiss them." Trina said.

She showed a video of an aboriginal who was more well-spoken than Lee was accustomed to an aboriginal being. He'd seen Indigenous populations of multiple inhabitable planets. Most of them were on an imperial acclimatization program.

She paused the video to show the half-formed crop circle.

"The one who did the extraction was working under par if they executed the marker wrong."

"I have a report on who's behind this. They say he used a laser to disrupt the navigation system."

Lee frowned. "You mean someone's been supplying Terrans with blasters?" He didn't like the thought of their being armed resistance.

"No, they used their native technology. A Terran laser pointer isn't strong enough to pierce the haul of our drones. However, it can transmit a bright light that disrupts the navigation system."

She showed this by taking out one of the laser pointers in question. "It's meant for an innocuous use. It just points to sections of presentations. But point it at people, and they could mistake it for a targeting laserscope. It can also blind a person if they aim for their eyes."

In her annoyance, she showed this on his person. "There have been people copying his technique on all our extraction sites."

"He wasn't able to record the incident in his field. But other farmers have put security cameras in place to do that. They record themselves resisting extractions."

Indeed, she played a series of videos of people shining lights at the drones during the night. Which often had to flee the scene. They couldn't do their work when their navigation system was disrupted by the lasers.

She brought up a letter received by their automated comments section on their web page. "Registering our trademark on Earth may've been a mistake. Someone was foolish enough to launch a copyright strike against an acquaintance of this man. He sold products with our crop circle design after we extracted seeds from his property. They wanted to stop it, but only made things worse. This alerted the Terran to our existence. The man traced the crop circles to our company."

"What's the man's name? We need to identify him to discredit him," Lee said. It was too bad the video got so much attention that they couldn't simply neutralize him. It'd look too suspicious if something lethal happened to him so soon after he made this post.

She flashed the name "Akweks" on the smart board.

He frowned. "What kind of name is that?"

"We found a Mohawk-English dictionary and the word means 'eagle.'" Trina told him.

"Why don't they just say 'eagle' and use the common tongue of their planet?" Lee asked her.

"That would be ethnocentrism and culturally insensitive," Trina said.

"It's too bad that Terra's empires never last long. They'd be able to impose a common language and diplomatic protocol on their planet."

Trina's eyes shifted upward for a bit, but she recovered herself before she rolled her eyes. This reminded Lee that she was chosen for her knowledge of indigenous peoples. Did that mean she was sympathetic to Terra's aborigines? It had to be investigated. Meanwhile, they got this indigenous man to deal with.

"The best tactic is to plant an obvious fake video to cash in on the sensationalism of this subject. We'll make the rest look like they're faking their videos, too. Then the Terrans will never know what the truth is."

Trina's brows drew together. "Are you sure that would work?"

"It's a common tactic for this world's elites. They control the narrative they want to present to the populace. Make the dissidents look like extremists by planting agitators. Plant a few obvious charlatans should a clandestine project of theirs be exposed."

Trina rubbed her chin. "That may stop him from having new converts to his cause. However, what about his more devoted fan base? We need to end this sabotage of our extractions."

"Make sure they catch our plants using the laser pointers against earthen airplanes. I want social pressure put on them to stop this behavior. We can then lodge a complaint about the misinformation. It'll get their social media platforms to flag their videos, so it doesn't go viral again."

"We'll do that, but executing it will take time. In the meantime, our extraction quota will have to be lowered." Trina said.

This time it was Lee who wanted to roll his eyes."I can allow your quotas to be lowered for this quarter. Although I expect you to be back on schedule once we've dealt with this earthling."

"A quarter doesn't give us enough time to discredit this man," she sputtered.

"It is time to set a pattern of unstable behaviour with respect to the public. Once that's done no one will think anything is wrong if he goes missing. Not after they've heard about erratic activities from him."

Which was true enough. Trina didn't have the stomach for extreme prejudice maneuvers against this aborigine. However, Agristar could always keep that as an option.

***

Trina had a markup of a video of a choreographed drone flight set to music during the night. The Terrans thought they were points of light. Every time a laser pointer connected to a drone's headlights, it created a discordant tone. This ruined the harmony.

Lee couldn't understand the reason for this video. "You're better off having a subtext of light pollution rather than a music video."

Yet it didn't stop her from posting. She was convinced she knew more about how to handle Earth's social media than he did.

Someone took the video and created a new soundtrack. The laser pointer created a whoopee cushion sounds every time it struck the headlight of a drone.

"Of all the!"

On top of that, someone created a post of them mowing their own crop circle. It had the words *you have to go back* inside a circle.

Trina created an internet mob against them. They looked at it as a comment on immigration.

She smiled when the poster escalated things. *Illegal aliens can go back where they came from, whether they're from our planet or outerspace.*

She typed in a response herself: *That's a hypocritical stance for a farmer. Don't most of you use migrants for farmhands?*

***

The next quarterly report was excellent. Trina's report said: *We shifted people's attention to illegal immigration rather than our extraction sites,*

Akweks's influence has shrunk. I believe he has lost interest in the sabotage program himself. The last time he commented on it, he said, "It has gotten high jacked by right-wingers".

I suggest we stop sending drones to his Indian reservation. We don't want anyone to draw a correlation to our extraction efforts.

He now takes part in a seed exchange program for indigenous peoples. I propose that we have an outreach that extract seeds through these programs. This program would be a discreet way to extract heritage seeds from his climate zone.

She posted a link to a new page Akweks had set up. The about section had an interesting call to action. *My grandfather got carried away with his heritage seed collection. We need to downsize it. He's got stuff that we can't even grow in our garden zone and the storage shed is overflowing.*

The list of seeds was impressive. It basically covered most of the crop seeds they wanted to extract from Terra.

Lee rattled his fingers across his desk terminal. *We could practically close the office if we get those seeds.*

Not only that, it would mean that they might still have reasonable production for that quarter. Maybe even earn a performance bonus.

"Computer, find me an Agristar employee with an online presence in good standing. I want them to perform a transaction for me in one of its marketplaces."

Lee frowned when he saw the team of one human and one feline. Fortunately, the feline usually wore a human holoskin. He wondered how a feline had gotten assigned to a planet inhabited by humans. Most of the felines on Earth weren't sentient. A large, talking cat would generate too much attention.

Chapter 7-Extraction

A dog barked as soon as they parked their car. Felix shuddered at this. His holomask convinced humans' eyes, but he couldn't deceive a Terran canine's nose. Worse yet, even a human could smell him when his fur got wet, and it was drizzling outside. The hairs stood up on the back of his neck and in other places that could not be seen.

Marcus said under his breath, "Do you want to get out, or do you want to stay inside?"

"I hate dogs and dogs hate me. I can't be responsible for what happens to the client's dog if I step out," Felix muttered.

"Your nails look like they need to be clipped. Retract your claws." The holomask humanized Felix's appearance. Yet, it registered any changes in his actual appearance. It gave him longer nails when he extended his claws and made his hair look extra spiky when his fur stood on end.

Marcus lived with this. He needed indications of Felix's natural state when they were about their business. Indeed, they had to live with each other's quirks for the sake of keeping their jobs and health benefits. They weren't the only ones who used Terran treatments. Most of Agristar's Terran Branch personnel transferred to Earth for the sake of the health benefits.

"Did it ever occur to you that it's just as well if this mission fails? They can close the branch if we collect the seeds in this collection," Felix whispered. He petted his own fur to calm himself.

"You can always buy up a supply of cat wine, so you can use it to create your own formula in imperial space."

Felix gave a cackling hiss. "I've already done that. What I'll miss is the heartworm and flea treatment."

"Do you still need them?" Marcus asked him.

"I'm on my last dosage of the heartworm medication. The flea medication is a chronic care issue. There's nothing like it in imperial space. I've become accustomed to being free from fleas and the constant infections they give me."

Marcus gripped the wheel of the car. He closed his eyes. "You know I have a chronic care issue, too. Earth has its flaws, but I can't stay away from this planet.

Not when it's the only system that has medication for my problem. I can live to old age here, but I'll die within 15 years if I'm exiled from Earth."

Felix nodded at this. "That's what makes your breath and your body smell less sweet?"

Marcus nodded. "My body weight is in a healthy standard. Yet, not even a proper diet followed religiously is enough to keep my blood sugar within a healthy range. I need insulin for that."

The feline laughed. "Your health regiment is your only religion."

They both jumped when there was a knock on the passenger window. A heavy-set man spoke to them. It was difficult to know whether the heaviness came from fat, muscle, or bone. He was broad and barrel-shaped, so his muscle may not be picturesque but present. Being healthy helped a human's looks, but it did not mean that they were always beautiful.

"I don't know what's gotten into, Buster. But I'll take him inside the house, so he doesn't interrupt us at the shed," the man announced.

The dog's barking grew louder as it got closer to Felix's scent. Felix hissed at the mongrel. Marcus gripped his hand as a warning and stroked his soft fur at the back of it. They were in the car and hidden from sight. Marcus had to do this regularly with his partner, even if it looked odd to non-imperial outsiders.

Felix's fur flattened when the dog was in the house and out of view.

Then both of them left the car and got to work.

The man came back. "Sorry about that. I don't know what's got into Buster. He barks a lot when something gets him worked up."

"I trust we can proceed with the transaction now," Marcus said.

"Akweks Pine, my mother was in Mohawk language class when she had me," he said.

"Oh."

"Yeah. My grandfather wanted his own seed bank, and then he got carried away. He collected things we couldn't grow in our climate zone."

Felix's brows drew together. "He hoarded them?"

"I consider myself lucky he didn't start hoarding cats," Akweks laughed.

The comment made Felix's eyes narrow, and Marcus gave him a warning glance.

Akweks was oblivious to it as he led them to a hut. "Basically, he wanted to ensure that there were seeds of every crop he loves to eat. He said he wanted to make them available to farmers. He didn't want them to have to walk all the way to the Arctic Circle even though he couldn't grow them here."

Marcus smiled. "That's generous of him."

"That's one way of looking at it," Akweks said.

"How do you look at it?" Felix asked him. He pitched it to sound like he was interested. The best way to get a good deal was to know what drove the seller.

Akweks shrugged. "I think the prepper suppliers got my grandpa worked up, so they can drum up more sales from him. I've seen stuff like this happen to him before. Since he's gotten older, I have to protect him from predatory salespeople."

He opened the doors of a wooden hut to reveal a treasure that should've been in a secure vault.

"Look at this stuff. It's stuffed to overflowing. I've given some to the Indigenous Seedkeepers seed exchange, but it barely put a dent to it. It'd break Totah's heart to have it wheeled a way by the junk dealers."

"I've used Facebook to find people to take the seeds as long as they pick them up or pay for the shipment. It'll take forever at this rate," Akweks said.

He grimaced. "He wants me to take the seeds to my shed, but I said I'll only take the seeds I need for a traditional garden and white corn seed. I'm only one man. I'll perpetuate my people's heritage seeds, but I can't do it for the whole globe."

"We can make sure your grandfather's seeds are given to a worthy cause," Marcus intoned. Felix's ears twitched at this, but the holomask disguised most of it.

"We'd be willing to take the seeds off your hands, but we require a truck to do it," Felix said.

Akweks snorted. "No kidding."

"It'll take us a while to secure the truck," Marcus said.

Akweks's eyes narrowed. "How long is 'a while?'"

"We should be back at the end of the week," Marcus stated.

"The best time is the weekend. I have to work at the water-plant during weekdays," Akweks said.

"We'll tell you when we're coming," Marcus said.

Felix punched in commands on his tablet, but Marcus motioned him to follow him instead. He stayed still in confusion, but Marcus pulled on his arm to follow him into the car. He knew when he ought to wait until they were inside the car to speak.

"Don't we need to get the acquisition transfer form signed?" Felix asked in a low purr.

"Yes," Marcus said as he started up the car.

"Then why haven't we got it done now?"

Marcus smiled. "Akweks Pine isn't the owner of the collection. Neither does he have power of attorney over the owner's assets."

Felix jutted his muzzle out to gesture to the house. "Maybe not, but Akweks is his caretaker. Going over his head is bound to make him suspicious."

"It'll be too late for him to do anything by then," Marcus said.

***

They returned with a truck the next morning to call on the old man. He was sitting on his porch with his dog, who was unleashed this time. The dog growled at the two. "What do you two think you're doing here?"

His tone of voice made the dog growl louder and Felix arched his back. "Don't you dare growl at me, mutt."

"Buster has every right to guard his territory," the old man sniffed.

"We're here about the heritage seeds," Marcus said, hoping to de-escalate things.

"Then you should wait for Akweks, not show up when I'm home alone," said the old man.

The dog got away and chased them into the truck.

They closed it shut, and it clawed at the passenger side window, growling at Felix. "Stupid mutt."

The old man didn't do anything about it. Instead, he took a picture with his phone and punched in a text.

"I'll be so mad if he posts this outrage on Facebook." Felix hissed. "Run over that mutt,"

A ping came from Marcus's phone. He held up his hand to Felix.

The text was from Akweks. He saw a picture of Buster biting their truck's bumper. The caption read, *The deal is off. You're too creepy to do business with. I can't have you upsetting Totah.*

"No," he almost threw his smartphone on the dashboard.

"Uh," Felix asked.

Marcus showed the message.

"We can always use a proxy buyer even if we can't get it ourselves." Felix snickered. "Let the memory of those two creepy buyers fade. When it does, he'll accept a more plausible proxy taking the 'junk' off his hands."

Chapter 8-Plan B

"You need to vet your buyers better," Totah said.

"I had to broaden my reach from the Rez. Every Rez scone who is interested in your heritage seeds has already gotten a share of them," Akweks told him.

"You need to market the opportunity this presents you better. Try a new search term," Totah said.

You mean use the same sales tactics those gardening centres used on you? Akweks wanted to say.

What he said was, "What search terms should I use?" He asked him,

"Survival gardening. You can only survive on guns and canned goods for so long."

***

Indeed, most of the packages in the shed were survival garden kits for various climate zones. He posted, *We bought a survival gardening kit for the wrong climate zone. We can't take them back. We're willing to let them go for the cost of shipping.* It probably sounded too desperate. People assumed that something wasn't right with them if he accepted such a low price.

However, this was a token effort to satisfy Totah. His actual plan was to call a junk dealer to clean out the shed and haul it away. He could always take the seed to his own shed. Then he'd have the junk dealer haul it from there with Totah none the wiser.

He took pictures of them and put his list on Facebook to see if anyone was interested.

But those two prior buyers warned anyone who would've been interested about the dangerous dog at Totah's place. They posted a picture of Buster biting the bumper of the truck they used. The caption had the words *"beware of dog"* right under his post to market the seeds.

"Those two buyers I tried to contract with posted pictures of Buster barking at them in their truck. It shows up when I create a new sales post on the Facebook marketplace," Akweks told his grandfather the next time he came for a visit.

"It's their fault for showing up unannounced. Buster is civilized when I want him to be," Totah said.

"You let him run wild most times. It's not just white people being wimps. We've had people on the Rez ask you to tie him up," akweks grumbled.

"It's not as if these two can do anything offline."

Akweks took out the letter he received in the mail. He had a bill for repairs to the bumper on the truck that Buster damaged.

"There's a video record of Buster attacking that truck. They not only want payment for damages to their vehicle. They want Buster put down."

"Put Buster down? Why should I put him down when he was only doing his job? You don't want a wimpy guard dog." Totah's face flushed when he said this. "Tell them I refuse to give in to a frivolous lawsuit."

As soon as Akweks got home he thought, *This is becoming more trouble than it's worth.*

He logged into his feed and saw an online petition to save Buster. The post had a portrait of Buster looking super fluffy after a grooming session.. He clicked it and saw Totah had set up the petition and had gotten hundreds of sign-ups. *Buster's a good dog. He's a Rez dog and needs to be saved from systematic racism.*

Worse yet, he posted it on the marketplace, which also served as the community bulletin board. He posted links to Marcus's last post.

Akweks massaged his temples to dispel the beginning of a tension headache. "I'm going to have a flame war at this rate," he muttered to himself.

The massage wasn't working, so he went to his fridge and opened a bottle of beer. He had a pleasant buzz going by the time a new message pinged him. *I propose a ceasefire to this regrettable misunderstanding. I'll drop everything if you'll honor the first agreement. PM if you're interested.*"

He deleted the notice. Totah would be furious if he dealt with the ones who wanted to put Buster down. The seeds were his until he found a new owner. He tweaked his ad post: *I'll transport the seeds to anyone who wants them so they can avoid contact with the dog.*

He opened a fresh bottle, "This is my final effort to find people to pick up the kits."

"I did due diligence with Totah's seeds. I got as many people as I could to buy them and give them away to. If I must throw out the rest, so be it.

***

After doing some errands, he found that there were no takers when he came home. He posted an ISO from his smartphone app: *someone to haul junk out of a storage shed. We need to downsize a seed collection.*

He put the phone down, so he could put his groceries away when a ping went off.

I'd be willing to cart off your junk if I can do it without interference from that dog at the shed's location, a commenter said.

He checked their profile and saw they were a well-known junk dealer. So he saw fit to send a DM. *That aggressive dog is two plots down from my location. He sticks to his own territory, though he can get aggressive inside it.*

I can move the junk to my shed, so you can pick it up, but you must do it at the time we agree to. The last people I tried to trade with came at time I didn't expect. The problems happened because my grandfather was unprepared for callers.

He smiled at the response. *When should I come?*

***

"I'll transfer your kits to my shed," Akweks told Totah.

"It's about time. Heritage seeds are the best legacy I can give you," Totah said.

Akweks didn't tell him that he would just keep the seeds that belonged to their people. He wasn't keeping the ones for the entire globe. He didn't think they should compete with the world's seed bank. Especially with a garden shed they had a hard time keeping dry.

He brought over his truck to transport the seeds and loaded them up. Then he placed them in his backyard and covered them with a tarp. It was the only way to keep them out of sight. The junk dealer insisted on staying away from Buster but would deal with him.

He texted them when he unloaded the seed kits and waited for their response.

***

Before he arrived, the man had questions he asked with DMs.

Fields: So your grandfather transferred ownership of these heritage seeds to you?

Akweks: Yes.

Fields: What about that dog I hear about on the feeds?

Akweks: Buster isn't my dog. He's not on my property.

Buster satisfied his need for a pet, though he belonged to Totah, and he didn't have a dog on his property.

Fields: I know how things are on the Rez and need to check things out first.

Akweks: My only pet was a turtle.

Fields: Does he bite?

Akweks: He used to nip my fingers, but I didn't keep him outside. He preferred to stay in his aquarium.

Fields: Is he territorial?

Akweks: It doesn't matter anymore. He died of old age last year.

Fields: That's good to know. We can do business together.

The rest of the talk was civil.

Yet, Akweks checked the man's business reviews before he confirmed the appointment. He didn't want to attract a weirdo. Though the man may only be cautious because of past business on the Rez.

Yet, why would anyone steal heritage seeds?

"You need to understand. I am a junk dealer. That means I'm more than a cleaning company," Fields said when he arrived.

"Oh," Akweks stopped, suspecting he was pitching an upsell to him.

"I know places that buy used products for refurbishing. I also know scavengers who recycle materials that earn good prices on the recyclable market," he continued.

"And you don't have room for something that's a piece of junk?" Akweks finished for him.

The man guffawed. "No, I can find buyers for this. I don't want you to feel cheated when I resell it for a profit."

"I'm sure you're better connected than I am. My market's saturated," akweks said.

"I am," Fields shrugged.

He brought out a tablet and called up a contract for it. "I need a signature for this."

Akweks went through the form and looked at what the terms were. The bottom line was that Fields would collect the seeds at his own expense. However, he was free to resell it without giving Akweks a commission on the sale.

All Akweks cared about was that he didn't need to pay Fields anything. So he signed it digitally with the fine stylus Fields supplied him.

Chapter 9-Performance Bonus

Lee Astor looked over the inventory with glee. He chuckled as he looked over the assets they acquired. Marcus and Felix awaited his verdict on their performance evaluation.

"This is good. We'll begin the next phase and map the genomes of the heritage seeds. Then incubate samples of them before trademarking them in imperial space."

He had a piece of rough pottery on his desk. It had a rustic charm Marcus never thought Lee Astor would appreciate. Then again, Lee might've been seduced by his own curiosity. It'd been sealed the last time Marcus saw it, but was open now.

Indeed, Lee reached into the jar to withdraw a parchment with a hieroglyphic seal on it. Then he scooped out a handful of wheat berries.

Felix attended the evaluation without his holomask. His sharp ears perked up at the sight of the wheat berries. "Pharaoh's wheat?"

Lee nodded 'yes.' "This discovery justifies the entire extraction campaign on Terra."

"I foresee a high demand for the emmer wheat buds from the Nupt-Aegypt sector. The call it 'Pharaoh's wheat.'"

Marcus frowned. His performance bonus would be puny compared to Lee's. "It's their heritage stock, isn't it?"

"Yes, and they'll be interested buyers," Lee said.

***

"It figures. We do the work. Yet Lee gets the performance bonus," Felix grumbled back at their office when the meeting was over.

"We've got a job with health benefits that would cost a fortune back in imperial space," Marcus said.

"We'd collect bigger bounties if we were freelancers," Felix said.

Marcus bit his lip. "We wouldn't have the health insurance, though."

Felix spoke. "It's possible to buy health insurance as a freelancer."

Marcus laughed. "I could, but what about you? They have nothing for a non-human sentients on Terran."

"You can get pet insurance for me, so I can visit a Terran vet when I need to," Felix said.

"We're on good terms now, but what if we fall out? You wouldn't want your health insurance tied to me," Marcus said.

Felix grumbled. "That's another employment practice I wish would be adapted to the Imperial employers. The only reason they adopted it was because Terran employment laws required it."

Marcus smirked, "I checked the provenance of that Pharaoh's wheat."

"So it's a fake?" Felix asked him.

"Fake? Why would you suspect it's fake?" Marcus sniffed at the thought.

"Why else would you smirk like that?" Felix asked him.

"No, a collective of peasant farmers sells these wheat berries on the open market. Anyone who can pay the price can purchase a jar," Marcus said.

"What's the catch?"

"The catch is the concept of 'fair trade.' Most of the sale price goes to the farmers so that they can get a living wage for their labor." Marcus told him.

"How much does 'fair trade' cost?" Felix asked him.

"It adds more to the Terran price but is competitive with the imperial prices."

Felix nodded. "Ra would like anything that helps win his people's support."

Marcus glanced at him. "How do you know?" They worked together during most of their years of employment. He thought he'd know if Felix had such a major account.

"I've never met the Pharaoh or his ministers, but my family comes from the region. They employed us in the pest control division. Selling seeds was a step up from guarding the silos from rodents. Though it gave me the chance to learn what quality stock smelled like."

"I'm aware of Ra's policies because I lived under them in my youth. He's not perfect, but he strives to keep his subjects' goodwill."

Marcus nodded. "That's good to know."

Felix's nose twitched as Marcus sweat his adrenaline. He waited to see if it had the telltale sign of musk or urine. Marcus wasn't incontinent, but a trace of urine in his scent meant he was fearful and nervous. Excitement, which need not be sexual, made musk emanate from him.

Felix was glad when the sweat mixed with musk and Marcus's hands trembled, as they always did when he was excited. "Do you still have connections back home?"

"I'm on good terms with my family, though I don't visit or contact them often," Felix said.

"Can you cue them in to this find of ours?"

Felix glanced at him. "I wouldn't mind poaching a better performance bonus for myself. What can we offer them that Agristar can't?"

Marcus smiled. "We can acquire a jar and offer them a chance to trademark the Pharaoh's wheat genome for themselves. It'd never occur to Lee Astor to proffer this courtesy to them."

Felix answered with a cackling hiss.

***

"I have an acquisition that may interest you," Lee intoned during the holoconference.

They encased the wheat buds in a vase with hieroglyphics. It had a certificate of authenticity in both English and hieroglyphics. Lee kept the vase for the sake of the presentation.

He gave the signal for the technician to open the vase and reveal its contents.

Ra's eyes gleamed at the sight of the vase. "You raided a king's tomb for this?"

Lee held up his hand. "We purchased it from Terran peasants who preserved the seeds."

"Terran peasants hoarded this?" At least his anger was deflected.

"Ancient Egypt stopped being ruled by pharaohs. They probably didn't know where to deposit the seeds," Lee mused. "They had the wit to keep the seed stock safe, though."

"It's a wonder they did that much by themselves," Ra said. "Thank you for bringing this find to my attention."

He turned around and listened to the Minister of Agriculture. Lee controlled a start when he saw a muzzle on the minister, who was a feline. Most times, felines only guarded silos from rodents. Apparently, this feline worked themselves up to a position of prominence.

The minister was so dainty and graceful he knew the feline was female. She purred in Ra's ear.

"We have a similar offer from freelancers. They're offering to register the wheat's trademark for us. Can you top that offer?"

Lee grit his teeth.

***

Felix talked to Lady Farah in excited brees and chirps. This was how civil feline discourse was composed. Of course, feline conversation included scent as part of the body language. Though they adapted to telecommunications.

"So?" Marcus asked when the transmission ended.

"Sending a seedling of catnip to Lady Farah was ingenious. She's commissioned more from us," he said.

"That could mean a nice bonus, but what about the emmer wheat?" Marcus asked him.

"Lee made his offer and is giving them a week to consider it. He says it's an offer of first refusal."

Marcus grit his teeth. "We have to register the berries' genome before he does it for Agristar."

"We can't map it on our own," Felix said.

Marcus called up regulations on his tablet and then cried out, "Aha!"

"What is it?"

"We may not be able to map the genome, but we can take the trademark out of reach. All we have to do is apply for a Creative Commons license."

Felix's whiskers twitched. "What's a Creative Commons license?"

"You may create derivatives, grow and sell seeds, but not own the genome. The genome is common property," Marcus said.

Felix rubbed his chin to calm himself. "At least Lee won't get a performance bonus for our work. Do it."

***

Lee glared at the notice on his terminal's screen. He called in Trina who often diagnosed IT issues for him. She came to him within five minutes, but it felt like an eternity to Lee.

"Something's wrong with our equipment. Our registration for the emmer wheat trademark was rejected." He said.

"Did you submit the application correctly?" she asked him.

"I believe so, but you may know better than me."

She looked over his shoulder and scrolled through the error message. "Everything appears in order." She kept scrolling through the fields and then stopped at one that was marked with red glyphs.

"Let's see what comes up." She touched the section on the screen. The section popped up to create a field with more in-depth information. "Ah."

"Ah?" He frowned. "What does 'ah' mean?"

"It means your registration isn't being accepted because it's registered in the system already." Trina said.

"Registered already? How is it possible? Does someone already have stock built up in imperial space?"

She called up the certificate, "It's a recent registration. Someone placed it under a Creative Commons license last week."

Lee ground his teeth at this.

He rubbed his temple. "Is it still possible to make and trademark a derivative of it?"

"Of course," Trina said.

"Then I want a gene modification done on it, so we can trademark it ASAP," he said.

"The derivatives they envision are usually done with crossbreeding," Trina said.

"But there's nothing that forbids creating a GMO product based on the emmer wheat genome, is there?"

Trina laughed. "You may have something,"

Chapter 10-Health Benefits

"I don't see why you're so concerned about this. You're the one who wanted us to become freelancers." Marcus told Felix as they waited in their motel room for a job interview.

Felix's fur stood on end. "I wanted to build our own client base and save up money for the transition. I didn't expect to be terminated because Lee found out we registered those seeds before he could."

"Don't worry, we'll soon be employed again. I've got an interview lined up for us with the Freetraders Seed Bank Exchange."

Felix sniffed at this. "Their benefits aren't as good as Agristar's."

"Actually, the health benefits are better than Agristar's. It's the commission structure that isn't as good as we'd like it to be." Marcus replied, "A quarter of the compensation is in calories. You get an allotment of food compatible with your species physiology."

Felix's ears propped up at this. "Is that guaranteed?" Felix's interest was more than Marcus expected it to be.

"It's in all their employment contracts, even if working for food is a sign of desperation."

Felix hissed at him. "Spoken like a human who doesn't need special accommodations to get adequate service."

Marcus waved his hand. "I have to stay in the Terran system. It's the only place that accommodates my condition or has a treatment program for it."

"You've still got more options and I do. The Terrans can't be blamed because they don't have sentient felines here. However, you'd think the Empire would have more courtesy."

"The Terran vets keep you able-bodied, Felix. You were sent here to die of the heartworm that infected you. There was no treatment for it in imperial space."

"That heartworm medication is something that could be exported to imperial space. It'd make a good profit if I could convince them to service felines." Felix's fur stood on end.

"The Freetraders Seed Bank strives to be inclusive. You might talk them into importing the medication." Marcus told him.

"Indeed, you can include that as your pitch during the job interview. It'll show them you are aware of the opportunities in the region even if they pass on it."

Felix looked up at a gallery of crop circles on his tablet. "How come I've never seen their crop circles in the Terran farmers' fields?"

"They believe branding precious farm land isn't ecologically responsible. They have a more discrete way of pulling whatever they want out of the system." Marcus used his tablet to call up an online portal for a cryptocurrency exchange.

The glyph of imperial currency caught Felix's eye. "They accept galactic credits on Terra?"

"It's offered as a cryptocurrency. Its value is volatile. They can be traded for imperial grade electronics and equipment. They're formatted to be compatible with Terran technology." Marcus said.

"What do they get out of it?" Felix asked him.

"Terran currency to buy Terran heritage seeds from fair trade outlets."

"And the Terrans aren't aware of its true purpose?"

Marcus chuckled. "It's an open secret among knowledgeable Terrans. Anyone outside their clique thinks they're role-playing LARPers. Or else delusional if they know what these geeks are doing at all."

***

The Freetraders had an impressive branch on Earth. It was a casino renowned as a venue for sci-fi conventions. Awkward geeks looking for some world where they'd fit in attended the conventions.

A fit cosplayer dressed like an intergalactic slave girl caught Marcus's eye. "She looks like prime merchandise, but being chattel wouldn't be so glamorous."

Felix laughed. "I saw the movie. They forced the female lead to wear the costume and killed her captor for the insult to her honor. Fans have a fetish about her costume."

Some vendors were extraterrestrials who comported in the open without wearing holomasks. Their customers thought they wore costumes and prosthetics for the sci-fi fandom.

Marcus smiled when a geek muttered, "It's like being in an alien bazaar in space."

Felix almost laughed when he heard. "I wish they'd step things up and come up with some cool alien cuisine. All I could find was this dry and flavorless ration pack. It's like edible plastic."

Their friend snickered, "Are you so sure it isn't plastic?"

"I was told they formulated it to be edible for humans."

The vendors flocked to the buffet table during their breaks. They preferred Terran cuisine to their regular fare. Though some of the more censorious muttered about "degenerate gluttony."

The other attendees were of the tinfoil hat variety. He wrinkled his nose when a heavy set woman wore the slave girl costume. "Imperial space would find these people strange as well."

They saw some booths contained merchandise from outside the system. The conventioneers thought they were only souvenirs. Someone bought a thermal blanket and wore it as a cape.

Marcus sniffed. "I prefer Terran fleece blankets over imperial thermal blankets. They do the work just as well and have a more pleasant texture."

Felix shrugged. "I prefer the sensory blankets Terran quilters make for their pets. They embed catnip and lavender into the batting. That's true luxury to a feline."

Felix's nose twitched when they walked past the casino's buffet. "They're serving steamed sole and tuna lettuce wraps."

Marcus nodded. "They've got better hospitality than Agristar does. However, we're neither employees nor guests yet."

They went to their meeting coordinates and found out that it was a private dining area rather than an office. A beautiful humanoid woman waited for them. She wore a light floral scent that permeated everything she touched.

Felix took a deeper whiff and whispered, "She's a botanical, wearing a holomask like I am."

Botanicals could configure themselves into pleasing humanoid shapes, but were sentient plants. The more sociable members of their race spent all their time in humanoid forms. The traditionalists preferred to root themselves to the ground of agrarian planets.

She drank a smoothie that was probably a disguised fertilizer solution. Her botanical nature explained how her scent could be delicate yet persistent. She stood up when they entered the room, smiled, and held her hand out to usher them to the table.

"Order whatever you want from the buffet and the server will fetch it for you," she said.

She gestured to the wall panel that had a live feed of the buffet tables. "There are no rations here. You can eat as much as you want within a 45-minute period."

Marcus noted some Imperial citizens gaping at the selection of food.

"We've also got Terran vendors in the food court." She caressed her glass. "My favourite is the smoothie bar."

"We appreciate your generous hospitality, Ms. Gaia," Marcus said.

"A Terran once said 'there is no such thing as a free lunch,'" Felix said.

"Consider it a belated commission for sending work our way. We've got collectives that have contracted us to grow seed stock for Pharaoh's wheat. It became available to them when you put it under the Creative Commons license," Gaia said.

"We're pleased the jar we donated to the commons is being widely distributed," Marcus said.

"It's the cleanest specimen I've seen in a while. There are some clients who prefer to do their own genetic modifications. Though they want to start with a clean original sample. We supply that market too."

"Yet, The Pharaoh chose the Agristar derivative." Felix muttered.

"There is a collective of Nupt- Aegyptian farmers who want to grow their heritage seed. They commissioned seed stock from us," Gaia said.

"We've been in contact with the Terran, who provided the seeds. He says his grandfather is a 'packrat' and there are more heritage seeds he didn't know about. He wants to find good custodians for them," Marcus said.

Gaia nodded. "We can do this if the other heritage seeds are of the same quality."

"He comes from an indigenous tribe. They're known for having advanced agricultural techniques. They developed them before they were colonized," Marcus added.

"The seeds still need to be evaluated first before we commit to an offer on them," Gaia said as she sipped her smoothie.

"Orchestrating this evaluation will be a short term contract. We'll speak about a full time position if and when you successfully complete this task. In the meantime, you'll have access to our accommodations, resources, and office space."

A vein pulsed in Marcus's clinched jaw. He knew he couldn't negotiate a counter offer. He had to either accept or reject Gaia's offer.

***

Felix inhaled a blanket scented with a lavender and catnip sachet. It was meant for guests who came with their pet cats. "It's as good as the crafters' sensory blankets."

Marcus counted some items he had in his travel carry all. He gulped, and his scent spiked with a taint of urine. "We need to complete this transaction within six weeks."

"Huh? Why six weeks," he said.

"I only have six weeks' supply of insulin. I need to be on a health care plan by then," Marcus said.

Chapter 11-Orientation

They were scheduled for an orientation after breakfast, which was at the buffet table. Once again, Felix had to be creative about getting proper nourishment on Earth. The casino was pet friendly, and he used his expense account to get some premium cat food at the casino's pet store. He ate it as a breakfast cereal.

Marcus had to find a healthy breakfast from the buffet's offerings. Luckily, the buffet offered more than fast food to conventioneers. "Ah, an Imperial," the server said knowingly when he glanced at his spare frame.

They dropped their voice, "We can prepare a ration pack for you. Some Imperials find Terran food too rich for their digestion."

Marcus suspected the server was making work for themselves. Though he accepted the ration pack. His condition meant he had to be disciplined with his eating and drinking. Even if it wasn't enough to keep his blood sugar in range by itself.

Ration packs could be eaten dry, but were best when they were hydrated. The server said, "We have water, of course, but can steam the ration pack with a broth or milk if you prefer."

"Give me a chicken broth," Marcus said, wanting to see how it turned out. He was used to only using water, but the broth sounded like a unique twist he never considered.

"The Terrans are right. They say that the ration packs are too dry and tasteless in their native state," the server said.

"Terran food is too rich and fattening in its native state," Marcus countered with a sniff.

"That's true enough. Yet, a seasonal worker gave me the idea of being creative with the liquids we use to hydrate the ration packs. They even calibrated the food dispenser to their liking. They didn't want to 'accept whatever it's programmed to spew out.'"

Marcus snickered. "By coating its entrées with grease?"

"There are some dishes that include healthy fats. They can make a ration pack more pleasing, or you can add a beverage of fresh food products to it for hydration."

The cafeteria disguised the hydrator as a microwave, and it went off with a ping. He took out the pack, and Marcus's stomach rumbled from the savory smell that issued from it. He inhaled its aroma as if it were the bouquet of a fine wine.

"Your new techniques almost make the ration pack a gourmet meal," Marcus said.

"A true gourmet meal is too fattening to have, but there's no reason for healthy foods to be dry and tasteless. That's one thing Terrans taught us,"

Marcus's mind boggled at the thought of Terrans teaching Imperials anything useful. However, the server's words were proven correct. His entrée was infused with flavor yet not so savory it tempted him to overindulge.

When he got back to his table, Felix took one look at it. "I wish they'd put as much effort into rations for felines as they did for humans. I have to go to an upscale pet store on Terran to find something useful."

They ate their meal in silence and then went to their orientation. Gaia greeted them without her holomask this time. She looked the same, but her coloring was changed. Her smooth skin was green, and her fair hair had the texture of cornsilk with flowers in it. They could've been barrettes, but Marcus suspected the flowers grew from her head.

The conference room was full of exotic houseplants. They were healthier than what a human horticulturist could achieve. The flowers were bigger, more vibrant and fragrant under Gaia's care. As a botanical herself, she had an instinctive skill where their needs were concerned.

The scents they gave off were a profound aromatherapy. They had a certain sharpness that caused Marcus to strive to be mindful of what Gaia said.

"Take a seat," she said, gesturing to a semicircle of tables surrounding a podium. They did so, and she started her introduction speech.

"The concept of 'informed acquisitions' is one thing you must keep in mind. We don't steal growers' harvests and leave graffiti in their field as an added insult." She used a picture of a crop circle on the smart screen behind her.

Felix spoke up. "Does that mean we tell the Terrans about the Empire?"

"Only select clients know of the Empire. Most times, we use our cryptocurrency exchange to fund the purchase of heritage seeds. The Terrans need not know about us other than the fact we pay the prices they set for their wares."

Marcus said, "You said a few know of the Empire. Who would this select few be?"

"There are certain Terran horticulturists that specialize in growing certain seeds. We have to make them aware of the growing conditions for the seeds we intend to introduce to imperial space."

Felix spoke up. "I find it hard to believe that you need a Terran grower's advice on growing seeds."

She chuckled. "I found that hard to accept myself at first. Yet, now and then, I need advice from a Terran farmer on how to grow their native plants."

She waved to the screen to show a long grass growing near water. "Take sweetgrass. It's counterintuitive, but sweetgrass grows best when it's regularly harvested. Though one must not go to the extreme of overharvesting it. We believe it has a symbiotic relationship with the indigenous people who harvest it. It prefers their organic and manual means of caring for it. Sweetgrass flourishes best with personal attention from organics instead of automation."

This caught Marcus's attention. "We used an indigenous collector to acquire the Pharaoh's wheat. He's listed other heritage seed stock on Facebook. He needs to downsize the heritage seeds he found in his grandfather's basement. Could we make him aware of imperial space if we need it to score the deal?"

"I prefer you purchase the rest of his lot with a regular financial transaction. I want him to think he just made a sale, and he doesn't need to know any more."

"However, you're free to inform him of our mandate if you need to. Offer him galactic credits as cryptocurrency for the sake of the sale," Gaia told them.

***

They studied Akweks's listing with interest. *My grandfather became too greedy. He got seeds that are incompatible with a North American climate. Where can I donate these seeds?*

They gaped over a central shrine full of all the heritage rice seeds of Japan. *Totah has a penpal who also collects his people's heritage seeds. He wound up with over 200 varieties of native rice. It's suitable for every growing environment in Japan. The grower spent a lifetime caring for them, but he doesn't have any heirs interested in carrying on his work.*

Totah traded him some Haudenosaunee heritage seeds in a penpal exchange. We don't have enough room for them, but I won't throw them in the garbage. Does anyone know anyone who'd be interested in taking these seeds and caring for them?

Marcus tapped the screen at the sight of the shrine full of rice seeds. "This would interest the Star Nipponese. It'd be on par with the Pharaoh's wheat sale."

"Why hasn't this deal been grabbed yet?" Felix asked him.

"The provenance of these seeds makes for an odd story. One that's hard to believe if you haven't met this man personally. We know this man and his grandfather are prosperous and eccentric. No one else on Facebook does."

Felix rubbed his hands together, and that made sparks flow from the static electricity of his fur. "It's time for the junk dealer Fields to make an appearance to acquire this shrine."

***

Akweks answered the direct message Felix left him. *Thanks for the offer to haul off these seeds and find buyers for it. However, I found someone who's actually willing to give me $100 to buy this shrine.*

Marcus groaned that this. "A $100? That's a pittance compared to what it's worth in imperial space."

"Then it's worth our while to outbid the $100?" Felix asked him.

"Yes, offer $50 more." Marcus said.

"$50?" Felix repeated in disbelief.

"It's in keeping of with your disguise as a junk dealer who's willing to clean up clutter for him," Marcus shrugged.

Felix typed in the offer.

I'll tell Totah about your offer.

Felix whimpered at this. He stroked himself between the ears to help calm himself,

"There's no need to be nervous. What could go wrong?" Marcus asked him.

"It's not like the last time. He's not desperate to get rid of junk." Felix meowed.

Indeed, Akweks came back with a new DM within half an hour. *I talked this over with my grandfather. He wants to have a Zoom call to hear your plans for the seeds before he agrees to anyone's offer. He'll allow the one with the best pitch to have the seeds.*

Marcus patted his shoulder. "No worries, we can outbid any Terran."

"This set of Terrans is odd. It is difficult to tell what they want." Felix sniffed.

About the Author

Cathy Smith is a Mohawk writer who lives on a Status Reservation on the Canadian Side of the Border.

She is proud of her people's heritage, and has an interest in the traditions of other cultures. Most of her works to date have been based on the folkloric traditions she's studied. Science fiction and fantasy strikes her as the folklore of the modern age, and she considers both genres a natural choice for her own writings.

Please post a review if you enjoyed the book.

You can follow her at:

Wordpress: bit.ly/2e41qWT

Facebook: bit.ly/2dP3rXd

Twitter: @khiatons

Instagram:@cathy2891

Tumblr: bit.ly/2G3dEjo

Pinterest: https://www.pinterest.com/Khiatons/

Tiktok: bit.ly/3KoGwBf

Sign up to the Cathy Smith-Khiatons-I Write Substack https://bit.ly/4qATMGH to receive news and excerpts of new publications and promotions.